once we had a

HORSE

For my sister
ANNA ROUNDS ATKINSON
and her lively brood of children,
grandchildren and great-grandchildren.

Library of Congress Cataloging-in-Publication Data
Rounds, Glen, 1906–
Once we had a horse / written and illustrated by Glen Rounds. —
1st ed.
p.   cm.
"This new edition contains a revised text and full-color
illustrations"—T.p. verso.
Summary: Several children who live on a ranch in Montana spend
the summer playing with a gentle old horse which had been left in
their yard.
ISBN 0-8234-1241-5 (alk. paper)
[1. Horses—Fiction.]   I. Title.
PZ7.R761On   1996   95-25939   CIP   AC
[E]—dc20
ISBN 0-8234-1243-1 (pbk.)

once we had a
HORSE

by Glen Rounds

holiday house • new york

When we were quite small, we lived on a
ranch in Montana.

There were no close neighbors, so we seldom had other children to play with.

But one day a gentle old horse was brought into the house yard and left there.

At first we simply stood around and admired the old horse from a respectful distance.

But as we grew bolder, we found that
he would take bits of jellybread or
cookies from our hands.

Then one morning, before he rode out onto the range, one of the ranch hands lifted us onto the old horse's back and left us there.

At first the old horse stood still while we
clung tightly to his mane and each
other. The ground seemed awfully far
below us.

But just when we were beginning to
enjoy the feeling of being horsemen, he
took a few steps forward, and we fell off.

The high grass cushioned our fall so we were not hurt, and we spent the rest of the morning sitting on the porch steps discussing our adventure.

Every morning after that we followed the grown-ups about, clamoring to be put on the horse again.

However, we quickly found that learning
to stay on a horse's back is much more
difficult than it looks.

But with practice our balance
improved. And soon we began to look
around and enjoy the view from that
high perch.

Some days we rode all the way to the water tank before we fell off.

But we always did fall off, sooner or later. Then we either had to wait for someone to come and put us back up or find a way to help ourselves.

We tried climbing up the old horse's side
by hanging on to his mane, but this
proved to be very difficult.

So we tried piling things up to make a
high mounting block.

But that wasn't always successful either.

Later we found that the old horse would let us straddle his neck as he grazed.

Then when he raised his head, we simply slid down his neck and onto his back.

If one thing didn't work, we tried
another. Sometimes we could coax him
up to the fence or the hitch rail with a
pan of oats.

But we had no way to keep him from
leaving before we were ready.

We spent days trying to get an old
catch rope around his neck so we
could lead him to the fence whenever
we wanted.

We had watched the cowboys roping their horses, so we knew how it was done.

But somehow or other, the old horse
always managed to escape our noose.

However, we had plenty of time, and sooner or later we always found a way to get on his back. As the summer went on, we became better riders and often carried switches to hurry the old horse along.

Sometimes he would oblige us by trotting in fine style for a little way. But when he felt he'd hurried enough, he'd simply stop short, and we would slide off over his head.

We played with that old horse all summer, and he seemed to enjoy it as much as we did. When we were called into the house for meals, he followed us to the porch steps, then stayed close by until we came back out.

But when the first snow came, he was taken away to winter pasture, and we never saw him again.